D1309639

Where
Triplets
Go,
Trouble
Follows

Where Triplets Go, Trouble Follows

by Michelle Poploff

illustrated by
Victoria Jamieson

Holiday House / New York

Text copyright © 2015 by Michelle Poploff
Illustrations copyright © 2015 by Victoria Jamieson
HOLIDAY HOUSE is registered in the U.S. Patent and Trademark Office
Printed and bound in February 2015 at Berryville Graphics, Berryville, VA, USA.
www.holidayhouse.com
First Edition
1 3 5 7 9 10 8 6 4 2

Library of Congress Cataloging-in-Publication Data

Poploff, Michelle.
Where triplets go, trouble follows / by Michelle Poploff ; illustrated by Victoria
Jamieson. — First edition.
pages cm
Summary: Lily, Daisy, and Violet Divine, triplets, have different interests and like
to do things on their own, but they pull together when they need to, whether to
find out their grandparents' secret, create a good science fair project, or teach
their new dog to stop chewing.
ISBN 978-0-8234-3289-9 (hardcover)
[1. Triplets—Fiction. 2. Sisters—Fiction. 3. Family life—Fiction. 4. Science fairs—
Fiction. 5. Dogs—Fiction.] I. Jamieson, Victoria, illustrator. II. Title.
PZ7.P7957Wg 2015
[Fic]—dc23
2014017138

To Mary Cash,
with heartfelt thanks
for your inspiration and
encouragement

Contents

Chapter 1
A Divine Disaster

Lily Divine enjoyed writing poems and reading about kids in faraway places. On this rainy Saturday she was snuggled under her pink quilt with a book about an orphan girl in England.

On the other side of the room, her sister Daisy was tossing her baseball. The ball made a smacking sound each time it landed in her glove. Daisy was wearing her lucky blue baseball shirt. But Daisy wasn't feeling lucky today. Her baseball game was a washout.

Their sister, Violet, was lying on her stomach looking for who knows what in the closet. Violet was always losing things. All Lily could see were the bottoms of Violet's purple socks.

Violet, Lily, and Daisy Divine were triplets, but they weren't identical looking. They weren't identical thinking, either.

"It's got to be here somewhere," Violet moaned, backing out of the closet. She stood up and brushed off her clothes. "If I don't find that science test, I'll be in big trouble," she said.

"What's it doing in the closet?" Daisy asked.

"I failed my test again and tried to forget about it. So I threw it in there," Violet said, crossing her arms. "This time I have to get it signed." Violet stuck out her lower lip and looked at Daisy. "But my teacher didn't say who had to sign it."

"Don't look at me," Daisy said, checking out the window. Would it ever stop raining?

Violet turned to Lily.

"No way," Lily said, closing her book. She was just getting to a scary part and would have to wait and see what happened later. "But we'll help you look. Come on, Daisy."

"Okay, okay," Daisy said, setting down her ball and glove.

The girls began pulling shoes and clothes out of the closet. Violet's purple bathrobe was lying in a lump. As Lily picked it up, something crackled. She shook out the robe, and a scrunched-up ball of paper fell to the floor. Lily reached for it, but Violet snatched it away.

"That's it," she said, unfolding it and trying to smooth out the wrinkles. It still had the same failing grade written in red. "I'm never going to pass science. I'm just a big old failure."

"You're not old," said Daisy, tossing their things back into the closet.

"Har-dee-har-har," said Violet. "Tell me one thing I'm good at doing."

"Uh, you're good at losing things," Daisy said, lightly punching Violet's arm. "Like your toothbrush."

"It'll turn up somewhere," Violet said, lacing up her sneakers. "Besides, I had a spare."

"You're good at drama," Lily giggled. "In fact, you're the Divine drama queen."

"I'm serious," said Violet. "How am I going to pass science?"

"Extra credit," Lily said, reaching for her book again.

Violet stuck out her tongue. "Ugh, more science work?" she said.

"Never mind," said Lily, settling under her quilt for the second time.

Violet paced back and forth, shaking her head. "Our parents love science, and you guys always pass your tests. How come I can't get the hang of it?"

"Violet, Lily, Daisy," their mother called. "Please come down here."

"Speaking of our parents," said Daisy, scooping up her baseball.

Lily sighed and closed her book again. She patted it gently. "Don't go anywhere. I'll be back soon."

The girls found their mother downstairs in the kitchen. When anyone asked what their parents did, the triplets said they were rock stars. Helen and Herb Divine were geologists who taught at the local college. They studied volcanoes and rocks, and there were many specimens displayed throughout the house.

Herb Divine walked into the room. "That's settled, we're good to go," he said, putting an arm around his wife's shoulder.

"Go?" Violet asked, perching on a counter stool.

"I was just about to tell the girls," their mother said.

"Tell us what?" Daisy asked, tossing her baseball from hand to hand. She looked out the window. The rain had finally stopped. It was too late now.

"We got a call to examine some rocks and minerals that a geologist brought back from Canada," their mother said. "The research center is several hours away, so we'll be staying overnight."

"That sounds cool," said Lily, reaching for an apple from a bowl on the table.

"Not to me, it doesn't," Violet murmured.

"It's perfect timing, since Grandma Rose was already coming over," said their mother. "I called and asked her to bring an overnight bag."

Their dad clapped his hand to his head. "I forgot your mother was coming," he said. "I called my dad, and he's thrilled to stay over."

"Honestly, Herb, we don't need both our parents sleeping over," Helen Divine said.

"Yes we do, yes we do," the girls chanted.

"Well, there's plenty of food," their mom said. "My mother is bringing dessert."

Their dad chuckled. "My father said he'd bring dessert, so it sounds like a plan. I'll go fix up the couch."

"My mother will stay in the guest room as usual," Helen Divine said.

Lily nudged Violet. "What about your science test?"

Violet looked at the wrinkled test paper she was holding. She scrunched it up again and shoved it into her pocket. "I don't want to be selfish and ruin their day. This can wait until tomorrow."

Just then the bell rang. The girls ran to open the door.

On the step stood Grandma Rose, holding two bulging bags.

Coming up the path was Grandpa Dash, carrying two large plastic sacks.

"Hey there, Dash," said Grandma Rose. "It's nice to see you."

"Good afternoon, Rose," Grandpa Dash replied. "This is a most pleasant surprise."

Grandma Rose was the casual type, while Grandpa Dash was a bit formal.

The girls grabbed the bags and pulled their grandparents inside.

They quickly explained the mix-up as everyone hugged hello and good-bye.

"Save us some dessert," their dad said.

Soon Grandma Rose and Grandpa Dash were sitting around the table enjoying dinner while the girls filled them in on their latest news.

"This is a splendid treat, dining with my Divine granddaughters and their lovely grandmother," said Grandpa Dash. He raised his glass to everyone.

"That's very sweet, Dash," said Grandma Rose. "You always have such a nice way with words."

"And may I say that your rose-colored sweater is most becoming with your peaches-and-cream complexion?" he added.

Grandma Rose blushed. She took a long drink of water. "Well, thank you, Dash. I've been admiring your bow tie. It's quite, um, dashing."

Grandma Rose and Grandpa Dash chuckled.

Violet, Lily, and Daisy looked at their grandparents. The girls' heads moved from side to side as if they were watching a tennis match.

"Ahem," Violet said, clearing her throat. "I can't wait to see everything you brought for dessert." She gave Daisy a swift kick under the table.

"Ouch," said Daisy. "I mean, I can't wait, either. I hope you brought pistachio ice cream."

"I did," their grandparents said together. They rocked with laughter.

Daisy asked, "What are we waiting for? Let's clear the table and see what else you brought."

They quickly cleaned up and began unloading the goodies from the fridge and freezer.

"I brought plenty of fixings for some good old-fashioned ice cream sundaes," said Grandma Rose, handing containers to the girls.

"I had the same splendid idea," said Grandpa Dash, reaching for the strawberry syrup and whipped cream.

"Great minds think alike," their grandmother said.

Lily cut in. "I'm so glad you brought rainbow sprinkles and chocolate chips," she said.

"Indeed I did," said Grandpa Dash.

"Mmm, chocolate fudge, cherries, and mini marshmallows," Violet said, piling up the goodies in her arms.

"Oh, nuts, I forgot the nuts," said Grandma Rose, shaking her head.

"If it's nuts you want, it's nuts you'll get," their grandfather said, handing her a big bag.

Grandma Rose patted Grandpa Dash's arm. "Oh, Dash, you crack me up."

Violet rolled her eyes.

Daisy shook her head.

What was going on with their grandparents tonight?

Lily stacked bowls and spoons on the card table they had set up to arrange the toppings. "This looks yummier than an ice cream parlor," she said, standing back to admire the colorful display.

"It's perfect," Violet agreed. "Let's try everything."

"Ladies first," said Grandpa Dash. He stepped forward in a sweeping bow. As he did, he bumped into a table leg, which buckled. "Whoops!"

The toppings slid.

"Catch them!" Daisy said.

"Grab hold of the table!" yelled Grandma Rose.

Hands reached out to grab the dishes and bowls. M&M's and chocolate chips flipped into the whipped cream. Mini marshmallows and cherries bounced on the fudge sauce. Sprinkles and nuts flew into the strawberry syrup.

Grandpa Dash tripped and fell, taking Lily with him.

Violet and Daisy leaned over to help them up.

"My darling Lily, are you all right?" Grandpa Dash asked, pulling her in for a hug.

"I'm fine, Grandpa, but how are you?" Lily said, picking sticky nuts off their shirts.

"Couldn't be better," he said. "Luckily I have plenty of padding," he chuckled, tapping his bottom.

"Oh, pshaw," said Grandma Rose. "You're fine just the way you are."

Grandpa Dash's sticky-out ears turned red. His bow tie was covered in caramel sauce. There were

rainbow sprinkles on his mouth and chin. "What a disaster. I'm terribly sorry to have ruined our delightful dessert."

"No fuss, no muss," said Grandma Rose, helping him remove his bow tie. "I'll take this home and have it cleaned in a jiffy. And these topsy-turvy toppings will taste twice as good as before."

"That's for sure," said Lily. She plucked out a cherry floating in fudge sauce and popped it in her mouth. "Perfecto," she said.

"Let's get this slippery floor cleaned and then we'll continue with the festivities," said Grandma Rose.

Violet went to get the mop and bucket.

"Might I ask that we keep this dessert disaster just between us?" asked Grandpa Dash.

"What dessert disaster?" Lily said. "We have no idea what you're talking about."

Grandpa Dash's face broke into a rainbow-sprinkled smile.

Chapter 2
It's Not Fair

On Monday afternoon, Violet gave her teacher the wrinkled science test signed by her father. Her father had said he would help with her studying.

Just before class ended, Ms. Briggs handed out flyers for the upcoming science fair. "Everyone who enters a project will get extra credit," she said. "And a gift card from the Kidz Crafts Store will be given for the best project in each grade. Let me see by a show of hands who will participate."

Before she could change her mind, Violet's hand shot up in the air.

"Wonderful," said Ms. Briggs. "The sign-up sheet is right down the hall."

Then the bell rang. Science was the last class of the day, and Violet was looking forward to going home.

"Are you really signing up for the science fair, Violet?" asked Frostine Frazier. Frostine sat next to Violet and was a science smarty. She always peeked at Violet's paper when their tests were returned.

"Sure, why not?" said Violet.

"I'll tell you why not," said Frostine. "You're hopeless in science."

"For your information, I'm going to enter a great science project and get extra credit," Violet said, putting her books in her purple backpack.

"It will have to be the greatest project on earth for you to get extra credit, Vi," Frostine said, poking Violet's shoulder.

If there was one thing Violet couldn't stand, it was being called Vi. But this wasn't the time to get into that with Frostine.

"Just you wait and see, Frosting," Violet said, poking Frostine back.

Then Violet heard giggling behind her. It was coming from Frostine's friends, Haley and Kristen.

"You shouldn't bother," said Haley. "Everyone knows Frostine's science projects are the best."

"You mean, *were* the best," said Violet. She was sorry as soon as those words slipped out of her mouth.

"Quit ganging up on Violet," said a voice from the back of the room.

The girls whirled around. There stood Tillie, the quietest kid in class. No one had noticed she was still there.

"I bet you'll come up with a cool project," she said, giving Violet two thumbs up as she left the room.

The girls were too stunned to speak.

Frostine was the first to find her voice. "You'll never do a project on your own."

"That's right," said Kristen. "Your sisters will help you."

"I'm sure you triplets do everything together," said Haley.

"No we don't," Violet said, thumping her chest. "This is my science project and I'm signing up right now." She pulled on her backpack and started toward the door.

"Not before I do," said Frostine, elbowing Violet out of her way. "I don't need the extra credit, but I do need that gift card from Kidz Crafts."

"Don't be so sure you'll get it," said Violet, catching up with her.

With their jackets and backpacks on, Violet and Frostine tried squeezing out of the narrow doorway at the same time. They shoved and pushed and ended up getting stuck.

"Ugh," Frostine grunted.

Violet managed to wiggle her arm loose and tapped Frostine's opposite shoulder.

Frostine turned around, and Violet slipped out of the room.

It worked every time. Violet raced down the hall to sign up before Frostine.

"I'll get you back," Frostine called after her.

Violet grinned, glad she had beat Frostine at something. Now all she had to do was get her sisters on board.

Easy peasy, cherry squeezy.

Later that day, while the girls were up in their room doing homework, Violet waited for the right moment to put her plan into action.

Daisy stretched. "I'm taking a break," she said.

This is it, thought Violet, taking the flyer out of her backpack. She quickly folded it into a fan shape and began fanning her face with it. She sighed long and loud.

Lily looked up from the computer. "Why are you fanning yourself with that paper?"

"Oh, this old thing," Violet said. "I was thinking of maybe entering the science fair to get extra credit."

"That's cool, Violet," said Lily. "Now you won't fail science."

"Yeah, go for it," Daisy said.

Violet tapped the fan flyer on her arm. "There's just one itty-bitty thing," she said. "I need my two most favorite sisters to help me." She smiled her best sisterly smile.

Daisy and Lily looked at each other.

"We're your only sisters, Violet," said Daisy.

"That's why you're my faves," Violet said.

"Sorry, Violet," said Lily. I'm already partners with Brina."

"And I'm teaming up with Justin," said Daisy.

"I already told that bossy big shot Frostine Frazier that I have a plan," said Violet, plopping down on her bed. "She always wins at everything."

"You know, it's not about winning, it's about doing the work on your own project," Lily said, walking over to her sister. "We would have teamed up with you, but you were never interested in science."

Violet bounced off her bed. She threw the flyer on the floor and faced her sisters. "I'm your own flesh and blood, but you'd rather team up with strangers. And one of them is a booger-brained boy!" She marched across the room and pulled open the door. "You're nothing but traitors!" she called out, shutting the door with a bang.

Chapter 3
Strikeout

Frostine wouldn't stop bragging about her science fair experiment. "My project will save the planet," she announced.

"I wish it would save my ears," said Violet. She turned and flashed a smile at Tillie.

Tillie grinned back.

"Look who's talking. You should get going on your own project," Frostine said.

"You're right," Violet agreed. "I should get going." She couldn't get away from Frostine fast enough.

After school, she and Lily went to the baseball field to cheer for Daisy and her team. Violet was glad to take her mind off science and Frostine. They got good seats in the bleachers and waved to Daisy, who was warming up. The Eagles were decked out in their blue uniforms. They were playing against the Red Rovers.

The sisters cheered when Daisy took her position in left field.

Then Frostine and Kristen loudly clomped up into the bleachers and took seats right behind them.

Violet's heart sank.

"Danny looks so cute in his uniform," said Kristen. "I think he likes me."

"Justin's cute, too," Frostine said. "I asked about doing the science fair project together, but he's doing something with his friend."

Lily nudged knees with Violet. They knew who Justin's science fair buddy was, all right.

Though Violet would have loved to spill the beans, Frostine would find out soon enough. But right now, her sharp, bony knees kept digging into Violet's back. Violet inched closer to Lily. Frostine's knees followed her.

Finally Violet had had enough. She whirled around. "Keep your knees to yourself, Frostine," she said.

"Well, excuuuse me," said Frostine. "Anyway, shouldn't you be home working on you know what?"

Lily poked Violet. "Daisy's coming up to bat."

"Go, Daiseeeey, go, Daiseeeey," the sisters chanted.

Daisy lifted the bat over her right shoulder. She gripped it with both hands and bent her knees. The pitcher threw the ball and Daisy swung.

"Stee-rike one," the umpire called.

The second pitch was wide, but Daisy swung anyway.

"Stee-rike two," said the ump, holding up two fingers.

"Couldn't your sister see that ball was a mile away?" said Frostine, sticking her head in between Lily's and Violet's shoulders.

"She'll get a hit, don't you worry," Violet said, hoping she was right.

"What, me worry?" said Frostine.

On the next pitch, the tip of Daisy's bat finally connected with the ball. Daisy dropped the bat and ran, but she was tagged out at first base.

"Better luck next time," said Kristen.

"Just you wait," said Violet.

Daisy was usually a good fielder. But when the

Eagles took the field again, she missed some easy fly balls and pop-ups.

"Daisy's sure having a bad day," Lily said to Violet.

Violet agreed.

"How did your sister ever make the team?" Frostine asked.

The girls ignored her.

Daisy's bad day got worse. Later a ground ball went right through her legs. When she got up to bat again, she kept missing the ball.

Violet turned to Lily. "She needs to focus and wait some more," she said.

Lily nodded. "Wait for your pitch, Daiseeeey!" she called out.

"Stee-rike three! You're out," called the umpire. Daisy's head slumped to her chin as she slowly walked back to the dugout.

The girls cringed when their sister missed a high fly ball. Daisy ran far out for the ball. It bounced, and by the time she got it and threw it to a teammate, the runner was sliding into home plate. The Red Rovers had scored.

"Maybe the sun was in her eyes," said Violet.

"Hah, what sun are you talking about?" said

Frostine. "It's cloudy and getting chilly." She stamped her feet behind Violet.

Violet couldn't wait for the game to end. Still, she hoped something good would happen for Daisy.

When Daisy finally got another chance at bat, she hit a single.

Her sisters cheered.

A few minutes later, they held their breath as they watched Daisy stepping and waiting and trying to steal second base. When it looked like a good time to make her move, Daisy ran and slid but was tagged out at second. Shaking her head in disgust, she walked back to the dugout.

"What a show-off," Kristen said. "She should have waited."

Violet agreed, but would never say so.

It was finally the bottom of the ninth inning. The score was one to nothing in favor of the Rovers. If the Eagles didn't score now, the game was over.

Max came up to bat, and on his second swing, the ball connected with a *whack,* and he was safe at second. The fans in the home team bleachers stood up and roared.

When Justin stepped up to the plate, the crowd

chanted, "Justin, Justin, he's our man, if he can't do it, no one can!"

Everyone remained standing and stomping their feet. "Stee-rike two," the umpire called.

Justin gripped his bat tightly as the ball left the pitcher's hand. His bat hit the ball with a mighty crack. The ball flew up and away. "It's a homer!" the fans cheered.

Justin rounded the bases, bringing Max home. The Eagles had won by one run. The crowd went wild!

"Looks like your sister had a bat day," said Frostine, cracking herself up.

"She's lucky Justin saved the team," Kristen added. "Justin time." The girls continued laughing.

Lily and Violet couldn't figure out why Daisy was off her game today. But they had to defend their sister.

"No one can be the star in every game," Lily said. "That's why they play as a team."

"And the Eagles did win," Violet chimed in.

"No thanks to Daisy," said Frostine. "Come on, Kristen, let's go congratulate the boys."

Violet and Lily waited for Daisy to collect her gear. Then they walked home together.

"Everyone has an off day," said Violet. "You've had some really great games."

"Not lately," said Daisy, kicking at a rock. "Something feels wrong, but I don't know what it is. I sure hope I don't get thrown off the team."

"The coach wouldn't do that to you," said Lily.

"But I missed some easy catches, and I probably shouldn't have tried to steal second," said Daisy.

"Probably not," Violet said.

"Thanks a lot," said Daisy.

"I'm just agreeing with you," Violet said.

"Well, you don't have to be so agreeable," Daisy said, thumping her bat on the ground. "And on top of everything, last week Ms. Lamb had me change my seat. I wasn't even goofing around. Now I have to sit in the front row."

"My teacher did that to a boy in my class," said Lily. "It was to help him see better. And then he got glasses."

"I guess I squint sometimes," said Daisy. "But I don't need glasses."

"Maybe you do," said Violet.

"Uh-uh," said Daisy. "They'll only get in my way when I'm playing ball."

"Maybe you'll play better if you wear them,"

said Violet. "Dad wears glasses when he's playing tennis."

"You would look cool wearing glasses," said Lily.

"Can it, Lily," said Daisy. "I'm pooped and feeling crabby."

Later that week, Daisy got glasses with sky-blue frames. Lily was right. She did look cool wearing them.

Chapter 4
Snoop Sister

Daisy's dad showed her how to clean her glasses with a special cloth. "I've been wearing glasses since second grade," he told her. "I had a feeling one of my girls would need them sooner or later."

"I'm not crazy about wearing them," Daisy admitted. "But it's been easier copying stuff from the board."

"How about when you're playing baseball?" her dad asked.

"Well, I haven't hit a homer yet," Daisy said. "But everything on the field looks bigger. It's more fun now that things aren't fuzzy."

"I'm glad it's working out," her dad said. "It's fun having a daughter who wears glasses."

"It just gets annoying when they slide down my nose," said Daisy.

"I'll tighten them up for you," her dad said. "If they're still slipping, we'll take you back to Dr. Tal."

"Thanks, Dad," Daisy said. "This feels better already."

Her dad hugged her. "Have a great day at school."

Daisy had just been dropped off from baseball practice. Her glasses had stayed in place all day. "Mom, I'm home," she called out, closing the kitchen door.

"That's great, honey. Grab some fruit from the fridge," her mom said from the living room. "I'm talking to Grandma Rose."

"Send hugs," said Daisy.

"Will do," her mom said.

Daisy took a bunch of grapes and sat down at the table. It was nice and peaceful in the kitchen. The grapes were sweet and juicy. Daisy sighed happily and closed her eyes. She was daydreaming about hitting a home run when she heard her mom talking.

"Yes, it will be fun to surprise the girls," her mom laughed. "I can't believe you and Dash didn't think of doing this sooner."

Daisy stopped chewing and listened harder.

"Oh, yes," her mother continued. "They will be so thrilled."

Daisy didn't mean to be a nosy pots and listen in. Still, she wished she could hear her grandmother's side of the conversation.

"As long as you and Dash are available, seven o'clock tonight will be perfect," her mom said. "I'm sure the girls will remember this day forever."

Daisy had heard enough. She grabbed her gear and pounded up the back stairs to tell her sisters. Lily and Violet were playing a computer game when Daisy burst into their room.

"You'll never guess," Daisy said, trying to catch her breath.

"You hit a homer," said Lily.

"Better than that," Daisy said, tossing her sports bag on the floor.

"Two homers," said Violet.

"Even better," Daisy said, flinging her baseball cap across the room.

"Just tell us, Daisy," said Lily.

"Okay, here goes," Daisy said. "I heard Mom talking on the phone to Grandma Rose."

"You mean you were listening in," said Lily.

"Otherwise known as snooping," Violet said.

"I wasn't snooping," said Daisy. "Mom knew all along I was having a snack in the kitchen. So it wasn't my fault that I heard . . ."

"Spill it, sister," said Violet.

"Grandma Rose and Grandpa Dash are getting married!" Daisy said, falling down on the nearest bed, which belonged to Violet.

"What? How? When?" the girls asked.

"They never said a word," said Lily. "That's not fair."

"It's supposed to be a surprise," said Daisy, sitting up on Violet's bed.

"No offense, but I'd rather not have your sweaty

grass-stained self on my quilt," Violet said, waving her hands in front of her nose.

"It's too late now," said Daisy. "I'm already on it."

"Save your drama for another day, Violet," Lily said.

"Oh, fine," Violet said. They sat cross-legged on her bed while Daisy told them word for word exactly what she'd heard.

"We didn't even know they were dating," Lily said.

"Well, you know how it goes with older people," Violet said.

"No, how does it go?" asked Lily.

"Things move much faster at their age," Violet said, as if she knew a thing or two.

"Maybe we can help them plan the wedding," said Daisy. "We could bake a big cake."

"And we can be bridesmaids and wear fancy pink dresses," said Lily.

"I'm not wearing pink," said Violet.

Daisy bit her lip. "What if I heard wrong and they're already married?"

"No way," said Lily. "They would want us to be at their wedding."

"She's right," said Violet. "And that means Grandma Rose's last name will be Divine."

"Yay, we'll all be Divines," Daisy said. "But remember, we'll have to act surprised when they tell us tonight."

"Let's practice looking surprised," Lily said, opening her mouth and eyes as wide as possible.

Violet put her hand to her forehead. "Oh my gracious, I never would have guessed that the two of you were so much in love," she said, rolling off the bed, pretending to faint.

"Don't overdo it, Violet," Daisy said, pulling her up.

Violet sat back on her bed. "I wonder if Grandma Rose will be wearing a diamond ring. We'll have to sneak a peek at her fingers," she said, rubbing her hands together in gleeful delight.

Lily rested her chin in her hand. "It's just hard to imagine them getting married."

"They seemed to like each other when they were here for dinner," Daisy pointed out.

"They sure did," said Violet.

"But," said Lily, "we've never even seen them holding hands."

"Maybe they're shy," Daisy said.

"Our grandmother is not shy," Violet said.

"They did come together to one of my baseball games," said Daisy.

"You're right," Violet said. "It was after our crazy dessert party. They sat next to each other. I remember because I was sitting on the other side of Grandma Rose."

"And I was sitting beside Grandpa Dash," Lily said.

"Did you hear any lovey-dovey talk between them?" Daisy asked.

The girls shook their heads.

Lily snapped her fingers. "Wait a second," she said. "I heard Grandpa Dash say to Grandma Rose that he had something to ask her."

"Why didn't you tell us before?" Violet said.

"I think someone got a hit," said Lily. "We were all cheering and I forgot about everything else."

"Rats," said Daisy. "So you never heard what he wanted to ask her?"

"Sorry," Lily said.

"Looks like we'll find out tonight," said Daisy, stretching out on Violet's purple quilt.

"Oh no you don't," said Violet, yanking her off the bed. "Hit the showers."

Chapter 5
Surprise, Surprise, Surprise

Sure enough, that night Grandma Rose and Grandpa Dash came to visit. But they did not arrive together.

The girls were spying on their grandparents from the top of the stairs.

Violet whispered to her sisters, "Remember to act natural."

"Did you check out Grandma Rose's hands?" Lily asked Daisy.

"I sure did," said Daisy, tapping her glasses, which really did come in handy. "I can see them clear across the room. She's not wearing any rings. But she does have a cute silver bracelet."

"Never mind that now," Violet said. "Let's go sit down."

"Sorry, folks," Herb Divine said, coming into the family room. "I had to take a quick call."

He winked at his wife and nodded to the grandparents.

The triplets squeezed onto a chair that was not meant to hold three people. They were wiggling with excitement.

"Why are you all so crowded together?" their mother asked.

"There's plenty of room beside me," Grandpa Dash said from the couch. He patted the wide space between him and Grandma Rose.

"This is more fun," Lily said. She wiggled a bit too much, and Violet landed on the floor.

"Oops, sorry," Lily said, trying to stifle a laugh.

"No problem," said Violet, a little too loudly. "I'll stay here for now," she said.

Grandpa Dash cleared his throat. "My dear Divine granddaughters," he began. "I won't beat about the bush."

"What bush?" said Daisy, looking around.

Grandma Rose smiled. "He means we have some news for you," she said. "It was a surprise, but now we can tell you that we . . ."

"Are getting married," Violet blurted out.

"What?" the grown-ups said, staring down at her.

Violet quickly got up and squeezed back onto the chair with her sisters. It was squishy but safer.

"Why, no," said Grandpa Dash. "We . . ."

"Are getting engaged," Lily said.

"Oh my heavens," said Grandma Rose. "We . . ."

"Are dating," Daisy said.

"No, no, and no," Grandpa Dash said, laughing and slapping his knee. "Whatever brought this on?"

The girls looked at Daisy. "Well, for one thing, both of you were having so much fun last time at dinner," she said.

Violet joined in. "And then you took Grandma Rose to Daisy's baseball game."

"My car was in the shop," their grandmother said. "I wanted to see the game, so Dash kindly offered to drive me."

"But Grandpa Dash," said Lily. "During the game you said there was something you wanted to ask Grandma Rose."

"There was?" asked Grandma Rose, turning to Grandpa Dash.

"I did?" he asked, looking puzzled.

Now all eyes were on Grandpa Dash.

The tips of his sticky-out ears had turned bright red. He tapped his finger to his forehead, trying to remember. Then he smiled. "Oh, indeed I did, indeed I did," he said, turning to Grandma Rose. "I was going to ask you if . . ."

Grandma Rose leaned toward Grandpa Dash.

So did Helen and Herb Divine.

The triplets held their breath.

"I was simply going to ask if you'd had the chance to tend to my bow tie," he said. "Have you?"

The girls let out their breath.

"As a matter of fact, I did, and here it is," Grandma Rose said, taking it from her purse. "Good as new," she added.

"Thank you, Rose," said Grandpa Dash, clasping her hand. "I'm so very grateful."

"And I'm so very confused," said Daisy, scratching her head.

"So let's get this straight," said Violet. "You're not getting married."

"You won't be getting engaged," said Lily.

"And you're not even dating," Daisy said.

"Guilty as charged," Grandpa Dash said, holding up his palms in surrender.

All the adults began laughing. But this was no laughing matter to the triplets.

"Will someone please tell us what the surprise is all about?" Violet said.

"Let's just say you can expect a new addition to the family," said Grandpa Dash.

Daisy jumped up, this time knocking Violet and Lily to the floor.

"Mom, are you going to have a baby?" she asked.

"No way," Helen Divine said, wiping tears of laughter from her eyes.

Their father's face was practically purple from laughing so hard.

The girls turned to Grandma Rose.

"Don't even think about it," she said. "Dash, you'd better tell them before someone explodes."

The doorbell rang. "Saved by the—ha, ha, ha—bell," Herb Divine said. He stood up to answer the door.

"Wait for me," said Helen Divine, grabbing his arm. "That was hilarious," she said as they hurried from the room.

The girls still didn't see what was so funny.

Grandpa Dash explained. "Actually, this is serious business," he said, pulling a pen out of his shirt pocket. "You girls will need to sign some very important papers."

"What kind of papers?" Violet asked, crossing her arms.

"Adoption papers," said Grandma Rose.

"Did our parents adopt a baby?" Lily asked.

"Well, you see . . ." said Grandma Rose.

"Is it a boy?" said Daisy.

"Yes indeed," Grandpa Dash said.

"Wow, a baby brother!" said Violet.

"How old is he?" asked Lily.

"Actually, he's . . ." said Grandma Rose.

"Arf, arf."

Their parents walked back into the room. Herb Divine set a box on the floor. The girls ran over and knelt down. Inside was a gold-and-white puppy.

"He's the cutest ever," said Lily. "He looks like a little Lassie."

"That's because he's a sheltie," their dad said.

"Can we hold him?" asked Violet, softly petting his head. The pup licked her hand.

"What's his name?" Daisy asked.

"You'll get to decide," their mother said. "But right now there's someone here from the animal shelter, waiting for us to sign the adoption papers."

"That's what we've been trying to tell you," said Grandpa Dash. "Your new pup is a gift from us," he added, wiggling his ears.

"That's our big surprise," Grandma Rose said, opening her arms.

The girls hugged their grandparents.

"This is ten times better than what we thought," said Violet.

"A thousand times better," said Daisy.

"A million," said Lily, gently picking up the little pup. "Now, what will we name you?"

Chapter 6
Where Triplets Go . . .

Wherever the triplets went, the puppy followed. The only trouble was that the girls still couldn't decide on a name for their dog.

Daisy gently tugged her slipper from the puppy's mouth. She tried giving him a toy bone. "Our pup would rather chew on my slipper than his own special bone," she said.

"From now on, we'll have to hide our slippers," Lily said.

"And we can't leave our socks on the floor anymore," Violet said. "I already caught him trying to snag them."

"Mom and Dad said we have to be more careful

with all our things," Lily said. "We don't want him getting sick."

"The trouble is, he wants to chew on everything," Violet said. She rolled their dad's old tennis ball toward the puppy. He chased after it. "Who knew one little pup could get into so much trouble?"

"What about naming him Champ, Prince or Frisky? Do you like any of those names, little pup?" Lily asked.

Daisy set the dog down and he flopped over.

"I guess not," Lily said, tickling his tummy.

"How about Hotdog, Muffin or Bagel?" Violet said.

Lily pretended to snore.

"Now that we have a boy in the family, we could name him Hank or Frank, or Billy or Willy," Daisy said.

"What about Larry, Barry or Harry?" Lily said, giggling.

"Now where did that cute little troublemaker go?" Violet said, looking around the room.

"Oh, no," Lily said, jumping up. "He's gotten into our craft box." She quickly scooped him up. He was chewing on a red ribbon. "Give me that, you naughty boy." She stuffed the ragged ribbon into the trash.

"From now on, we'll have to keep lots of stuff on shelves," Daisy said. She hoisted the craft box onto a high shelf.

"And we'd better keep our door closed when we're not around," Violet added.

"Who knows what trouble our pup will get into, right, boy?" Daisy said. She tried cuddling the pup, but he squirmed out of her arms.

The girls laughed as he chased the tennis ball around the room. When it rolled under Violet's bed, the puppy tried going after it.

"You can't go under there, little guy," Lily said, reaching for him. "We don't want you getting stuck."

Violet reached under the bed, stretching her arm out as far as it could go. "I can't get it," she said. "Help me pull the bed away from the wall."

The girls pulled the bed away and Daisy reached down and brought up the ball, which had some dust on it. "Oh, gross," she said.

"It's just a little dust," Violet said.

"That's not the gross part," Daisy said. "Check it out."

Violet peeped over. "Wow, it's my old toothbrush." She picked up the purple toothbrush.

"Eew, Violet," Lily said. "Get rid of it. It's all covered with germs and icky bits."

"I told you I'd find it," Violet said, waving it near Daisy's face. "Heh, heh, heh. Maybe I'll use it for my science project," she said in a witchy voice.

"Get that gross thing out of my sight," Daisy said, batting it away.

"That makes two of us," said Lily.

"Ruff, ruff."

"Make that three," Daisy said.

Lily picked up the puppy and kissed the top of his head. "We love you even when you get into trouble, trouble, trouble," she said, putting him down.

"*Arf, arf.*"

"It sounds like he's answering you," said Daisy.

"Yeah," said Violet. "Maybe he thinks Trouble's his name."

The girls looked at each other. Then they looked at their dog.

"Let's give it a try," said Daisy.

Lily walked to the other end of their attic room. "Here, Trouble," she called, patting her leg. "Come here, Trouble."

"*Arf, arf.*" Trouble trotted over to Lily.

She cuddled him in her arms. "Good boy, Trouble," she said.

Trouble wagged his tail.

"Let's tell Mom and Dad we finally have a name for our dog," Daisy said.

The triplets got going.

Trouble followed.

Chapter 7
Sticky-Out Ears

Violet was in a panic about her science project. It was mainly because she still didn't have one. At school, Frostine was stepping on Violet's last nerve. She wouldn't stop nagging her. Violet insisted it was a secret. And it was, even from Violet.

The girls had finished taking Trouble for a walk and were playing with him in the backyard.

"I just can't get started on my project," Violet groaned, flopping down on the grass. "I stink at science."

Lily was trying to get Trouble to roll over. She circled a dog treat above his head. "Come on, Trouble," she said. "Roll over, that's a good boy."

"You'd think I'd get some help from my own sisters," Violet complained. "Triplets are supposed to stick together."

"All right, all right. Your drama is driving me crazy," said Lily. "Brina and I are doing a project about how plants use sunlight to make energy that helps them grow. Maybe you could do a different project with plants or flowers."

"Plants are boring," said Violet, turning to Daisy.

"We're doing a project on rockets," Daisy said.

"Rockets!" Violet shouted. "Since when do you know anything about rockets? You're only doing it because you like Justin."

"I do not like him," Daisy shot back. "We just play baseball together."

"Rockets are even more boring," Violet grumbled.

Lily and Daisy nodded to each other and flared their nostrils at Violet.

"Cut it out," she said, throwing grass at them. "How come Mom and both of you can flare your nostrils and I can't?"

Lily shrugged, pulling bits of grass out of her hair. "I guess it's the same reason why you, Daisy and Mom have brown hair and I don't," she said.

"But you and Dad have freckles and blond hair," Violet said.

"And only Dad and I wear glasses," said Daisy. "So la-dee-da." She threw a squeaky rubber toy across the yard. "Fetch it, boy."

Trouble scampered after the toy.

"You don't have to brag about it," Violet huffed. "Just because . . . hey, wait a second," she said, a flicker of a smile appearing on her face. "I can sort of wiggle my ears a little, just like Dad and Grandpa."

Their father and grandfather had large sticky-out ears. Sometimes they wiggled them just for fun. It was okay for them. But Violet was sensitive about her ears, which stuck out a little. She thought they were big and ugly. Grandpa Dash said it was a Divine family trait and she should be proud of it. But Violet didn't think there was anything the least bit divine about her ears. She covered them with her hair. And she had never told anyone before that she could wiggle them.

"Wiggle your ears, just this one time," said Lily.

Why, oh, why had she blurted out this secret? "Okay, but just this once." Violet sighed, pushing her hair behind her ears and wiggling them a little bit.

"That's awesome," said Daisy.

"Don't tell anyone. I'm never doing it again," Violet said, reaching for Trouble, who had returned with the toy and dropped it at her feet. She stroked his silky ears, and they quivered.

"It looks like Trouble's wiggling his ears," said Daisy. "He has the same Divine trait as you do."

Violet laughed. "And he has blue eyes like us."

"He's a true-blue Divine," said Lily.

Trouble rested by Violet's side. She gave him a brisk back rub. "I wonder if he has brothers and sisters and if they look exactly alike," Violet said, gazing at her sisters. That's when it hit her. It had been staring her in the face all along. She snapped her fingers. "I've got it! I've got an idea for my science project," she said, tossing the soggy toy in the air.

"*Ruff, ruff,*" Trouble barked, chasing after it.

"That's great! What is it?" Daisy asked.

Violet grinned. "I'm going to do a project about the genes we get from Mom and Dad."

"What jeans?" said Daisy. "Mom and Dad's jeans wouldn't fit us."

"I don't mean those kind of jeans," Violet said, rolling her eyes. "I mean the kind of genes our parents pass on to us."

"I get it," said Lily. "You mean like getting brown hair from one parent or blue eyes from another?"

"Exactly right," said Violet, growing more excited.

"Grandma Rose says I have Mom's nose," Lily said, laughing.

Daisy agreed. "I see what she means. It's the same shape. And my middle toes are longer than my big toes, just like Mom's," she said.

"Hmm," said Violet. "My nose is a different shape than both of yours and I don't have that toe stuff going on."

"That's why we're not identical," said Lily. "We each have some different genes from our parents."

THE DIVINE TRIPLETS GENE AND TRAIT CHART

NAME	HAIR COLOR	EYE COLOR	FLARES NOSTRILS
Violet	brown	blue	no
Lily	blond	blue	yes
Daisy	brown	blue	yes
Mom	brown	blue	yes
Dad	blond	blue	no
Grandma Rose	brown	blue	no
Grandpa Dash	gray	green	no

"Too bad I didn't get their science genes," Violet said. "Then I wouldn't be in this mess." But now that she had a plan, she wouldn't worry about Frostine bugging her.

"But you did get the ear-wiggling gene," said Daisy.

"Don't remind me," Violet said, frowning. "I'm definitely not including that in my project. That's private family business."

"Speaking of your project, you'll have to write a report," Daisy said.

"Oh, whoop-dee-do," said Violet, twirling her finger in the air.

WEARS GLASSES	FRECKLES	WIGGLES EARS
no	no	no
no	yes	no
yes	no	no
no	no	no
yes	yes	yes
no	no	no
yes	yes	yes

"But you can also draw a chart showing the things we talked about," said Lily.

Violet brightened up. "Yeah, that would be cool," she said. "But you're better at drawing, so will you help me? Pretty please," she added.

"You have to do the work," Lily said. "It's your science project."

"And you'll get the extra credit," Daisy said.

"*Arf, arf,*" barked Trouble. He had dug up some dirt, and his paws were all muddy.

"Then I guess I'll get going on my ginormous project," Violet said, standing up. "And while I'm at it, you guys better clean that cruddy mud off our dog before you bring him inside and get into trouble." Then she ran off.

Once Violet got going, she was on a roll. She decided to include her grandparents in her chart. She pasted pictures of each family member next to his or her name.

The next day, Violet showed her sisters the chart.

"Why did you write 'no' next to your name under 'wiggles ears'?" Daisy asked.

"I told you, it's private," said Violet. "Now I have to write my report."

"What will you say?" asked Lily.

"I'll say I'm the oldest and that we're not identical," she said. "Then I'll write about the genes we got from our parents and some different family traits."

"You can also write that I like playing baseball," said Daisy.

"And say I like reading and writing poems," added Lily.

"Don't tell me what to do for my project," said Violet. "Go work on your own stuff."

Then she wrote down exactly what they had said.

Chapter 8
Eggs-cuse Me

On the day of the science fair, Violet felt like she could hear her heart pounding in her ears. Her stomach was full of boxing butterflies. She wore her favorite black leggings, purple shirt, and matching headband. Her hands shook as she brushed her hair in front of her ears. Daisy and Lily didn't have anything to worry about. They had done science projects before, and they had partners. Violet had never felt more alone.

Their father dropped them off at the school. "Good luck with your projects," he said. "We'll check in on you later."

When the girls walked into the lunchroom,

there were dozens of kids already setting things up at their tables.

Lily tucked her pink blouse into her skirt. Someone called her name. "There's Brina," Lily said, picking up her project bag. "I'll see you guys later."

Daisy wore jeans and a blue sweater that matched her glasses. "I have to get going," she said. "I'm meeting Justin by the water fountain."

"Right," said Violet. "You'd better get rocking with your rockets."

Violet turned and bumped into the one person she didn't want to see. It was none other than mean Frostine Frazier.

"I can't believe you actually showed up with a project," said Frostine, hands on her hips. She snatched the chart from Violet's hands. "Hmm," she said giving it the once-over. "So this is the big secret project you've been working on," she said. "It's no big deal."

"It's just part of my project," Violet said, pulling the poster back. "I also did a report," she added, keeping the folder close to her chest.

Frostine flicked her long, perfectly styled blond hair over her shoulder. "Well, my eggs-cellent project is going to win for sure," she said, getting up into Violet's face. "Kidz Crafts, here I come."

Phew. Violet wanted to step back, but she didn't budge. "Who cares," she said. "I'll still get eggs-tra credit for my project. That's all I care about." Then she stepped back. "By the way, did you have eggs for breakfast?"

"Eggs-actly," said Frostine. "How did you know?"

"For one thing, you have egg breath, and for another, there's some on your shirt," Violet said, pointing to Frostine's left shoulder.

Frostine looked at the icky egg stain on her sparkly red top. She scrunched up her face, looking as if she had eaten a sour pickle.

"I guess you will win for going the eggs-tra mile," Violet said. "Now, if you'll eggs-cuse me, I have to go set up my project." Although Violet's legs felt like they were made of jelly, she carefully carried her project and managed to make her way to table 19.

She propped the large poster board chart up against a tall stack of lunch trays. Then she placed her report on a little easel. "Looking good," she whispered to herself. Then she took a deep breath and stood behind her project, answering questions as kids, teachers and parents came by.

When Violet had a break from visitors, she looked around for Lily and Daisy. Their tables were on the other side of the room. She would have liked to visit them and see some other displays, but she couldn't leave her project all by its lonesome self.

Then Tillie stopped by. "Hey, Violet," she said, studying the chart. "Your project is definitely one of the best."

"Really? Thanks," said Violet. "What else have you seen?"

"I saw some projects about the planets and the weather."

"Ho-hum, boring," Violet said, pretending to yawn.

"I also saw your sisters' projects," Tillie said. "How come you're not working together?"

"Oh, um, they thought it might be interesting to work with other people this time," Violet replied. "We don't do everything together."

"Well, you're brave doing a project on your own," said Tillie. "I think it's cool."

Violet hadn't thought of it that way. "Did you do a project?"

Tillie shook her head. "I didn't want to do one by myself," she said.

Violet knew just how she felt. Then she had an

idea. "Would you like to come over and see our new puppy?"

"Sure," Tillie said, smiling. "We got a dog last year."

"Wow," Violet said. "I'll ask if you can bring him to our house."

"She's a girl," said Tillie. "But she likes boy dogs."

"That will be fun," Violet said, moving behind the table.

"Speaking of boys, the other good project I saw was the Schnitzer brothers' electrical display," said Tillie.

"I bet that's a shocker," Violet said.

The girls were still laughing when Lily and Daisy walked over.

"We came to see how you were doing," Lily said, adjusting Violet's chart a bit.

"Our partners are watching our projects," Daisy said, flipping through Violet's report.

Daisy probably didn't mean anything by it, but her words stung. Still, Violet stood strong. "I'm doing just fine," she said. "I like being on my own."

"See you later," Tillie said, turning to Violet. "By the way, here come those Schnitzer boys."

"I hope they don't set off any sparks," Violet said.

Sheldon Schnitzer was a grade ahead of the girls.

Alvin Schnitzer was in Lily's class and played third base for the Eagles.

"Check this out, dude," Sheldon said, pointing to the poster board chart.

Alvin looked from Violet to Lily to Daisy. "If you guys, I mean girls, are triplets, how come you don't look exactly alike?" he asked.

"It's because we're not identical," said Daisy.

Violet tapped Daisy's shoulder. "I'll take over, thank you very much," she said. She wasn't going to let her sisters horn in on her project. Violet turned to Alvin. "Actually, it's all here in my report," she said, pointing to her purple folder. "And my chart shows some things about our genes and traits. As you can see, some are the same and some are different."

"That's kind of cool," Alvin said. "Were you all born at the same time?"

Violet licked her dry lips. "Not exactly," she said. "I was born first."

"I was born five minutes later," Lily said, moving next to Violet.

"And I was born ten minutes after Violet, but five minutes after Lily," Daisy said, stepping to Violet's other side.

Even though this was her own project, Violet sort of liked having her sisters standing by her side.

"Do you have to share everything?" Alvin asked.

"Well, besides sharing parents, grandparents, and our dog, we share things like our computer, books and games," Violet said.

"But we have loads of things that just belong to each of us," Daisy said.

"Like our toothbrushes," Violet said.

The boys laughed as some more people walked over, including Violet's science teacher.

"We also like different kinds of clothes and colors," Violet continued. "We're not matchy-matchy."

"I bet you don't get to have your own room," Sheldon said.

"We have the entire attic all to ourselves," said Violet.

"Cool," some other kids said, nodding their heads.

"Well, I'm still glad I'm not a triplet," said Sheldon.

"That makes three of us," said Lily, flaring her nostrils.

Violet and Daisy looked at Lily in surprise.

"For your information, Sheldon Schnitzer," Violet said, linking arms with her sisters, "we love

being triplets. We're fine about doing some stuff together and other things on our own. It's all here in my report."

Sheldon clammed up.

"That was cool," a boy said to Lily. "You flared your nostrils, just like it says on the chart."

"I can do it, too," said Daisy.

The kids hooted as Daisy and Lily flared their nostrils at them.

"What about you?" Sheldon asked Violet.

"Uh, no," Violet said. "As I wrote in my report, triplets don't always look exactly alike, or have all the same genes, traits or interests."

Sheldon ran his finger across Violet's row on the chart. His finger stopped at the word "no" under "wiggles ears."

He laughed. "I can do that," he said.

"Prove it," another kid said.

Sheldon wiggled his ears. The kids clapped. Sheldon smirked at Violet.

"Maybe you're related to the triplets," a boy said.

"No way," said Sheldon, checking next to Lily's and Daisy's names. "Anyway, none of them can wiggle their ears."

Without turning, Violet knew her sisters were looking at her.

"Okay, okay," she said, as if talking to herself. Slowly she pushed her purple headband behind her ears.

Violet closed her eyes, counted to three and wiggled her ears.

"Awesome, check that out!" The kids whistled and cheered.

Sheldon reached out and high-fived Violet. "That was cool," he said. "Now you have to fix your chart."

"I guess I do," Violet said, grinning. She even forgot to brush her hair forward again.

"But we're still not related," Sheldon said.

"Absotootalootly not," said Violet.

Violet's teacher nodded and smiled.

"Triplets rule!" said Lily.

"Now you'd better get back to your projects," Violet said.

"I wish we didn't have to go back," Daisy groaned.

"We didn't get the chance to tell you," Lily said. "Frostine's table is near ours and her project on air pollution stinks of rotten eggs." Lily held her nose.

"She sure proved she's good at creating air pollution," said Daisy. "And you should have seen the look on her face when she saw I was Justin's partner. The stinky eggs were almost worth it."

Violet laughed. "Well, my project was worth it," she said. "Now I'll get the extra science credit."

"Admit it, Violet," said Lily. "Sometimes science can be cool."

"I never even thought of this as science," Violet said.

"Maybe you'll be a scientist someday," said Daisy, flaring her nostrils at her sister.

"Don't be ridonculous," Violet said, wiggling her ears in return.

Chapter 9
Puppy Love

Trouble had settled into his new home with the Divines. He was a playful and happy dog. The girls enjoyed taking turns walking, feeding and brushing him. They liked teaching him tricks, and Trouble was always ready to play catch, fetch and tug-of-war with them. At night Trouble slept with Lily. The girls said he was like Goldilocks, searching for the perfect bed. Daisy kicked her legs, and sometimes Violet snored. But Lily slept peacefully. Her bed was just right.

Lily had already taught Trouble to sit, stay, and obey other simple commands. "Look how smart Trouble is," she said, showing her family Trouble's latest trick. She stood up and placed a ball at her feet. "Take a bow, Trouble," she said.

Trouble brought his front end close to the ground, resting his chest on the floor. He lifted his tail in the air.

The Divines cheered for Trouble, who wagged his tail.

"Trouble's the perfect addition to our family," their dad said.

"Still, the one thing we need to work on is getting Trouble to stop chewing on things he's not supposed to chew," their mother said.

"Like my loafer, for example," their father said.

"And the wooden legs of the plant stand," their mother added.

"Don't forget the cover of our getting-to-know-your-dog book," said Daisy.

"We've been trying, but nothing seems to work," said Violet.

"Maybe he needs professional help," said Lily. "We can take him to a dog training school."

"Those schools are very expensive," their mother said. "We'll all just have to try harder. We don't want Trouble chewing on something that could get caught in his throat or stomach."

"Did you hear what Mom said, Trouble?" Daisy

asked. She grabbed his tug-of-war rope, and Trouble pulled at the other end with his teeth. Everyone enjoyed the show.

But Lily was worried about Trouble's chewing problem. What if they couldn't get him to stop and they had to give him away? Lily shuddered and shook her head, trying to get rid of that horrible thought. She went up to her room, reached under her pillow, and pulled out an ad from the weekly town newspaper. Lily liked reading the paper. The ad she'd kept was from the Dandy Dog Training School, which offered expert dog

training. But the part that caught her attention was about the Best Pet Contest. All you had to do was write a poem about your dog and send it in with his or her picture. One of the prizes was five free training lessons. If Lily won that prize, Trouble's chewing problem would be solved.

Lily often wrote poems for her parents, for her sisters and just for fun. She had never written a poem for a contest. As long as she didn't have to read her poem aloud, she would be fine. She decided not to mention the contest to anyone. It was hard keeping a secret from her sisters, but she would try. The deadline was just a few days away. Lily reached for her pink pad and began writing.

Our dog is named Trouble, but do not fear—
To the Divines, he is very dear.
He plays fetch and catch and brightens our day.
Then he takes us for walks and leads the way.
We love you, Trouble, oh, yes, we truly do.
Even when you eat the things you shouldn't chew.
When you're away from us, we're blue.
Oh, Trouble, we love you!

Lily rewrote the poem very neatly and chose a picture of Trouble from the pile on her desk.

Downstairs, she found a stamp and envelope and sealed everything up. Before she could change her mind, she ran to the mailbox on the corner and put the envelope inside it.

The next week, there was mail for Lily from the Dandy Dog Training School.

"What's it about?" asked Daisy.

"Hurry up and open it," said Violet.

Lily did. She quickly read the letter, then dropped it on the floor.

Violet picked it up and read it out loud.

The letter said that Lily's poem was a finalist in the contest. She was invited to come to the Dandy Dog Training School on Saturday to read her poem. Her dog and family were also invited.

"Wowza, that's so cool, Lily," said Daisy.

"We had no idea you'd entered a contest," Violet agreed.

"We're so proud of you, Lily," their dad said, wrapping her in a hug. "Mom will be thrilled when she gets home."

Trouble barked and wagged his tail.

But Lily stood glued to the spot.

"What's wrong?" said Daisy.

"I can't do it," said Lily.

"You already did, sweetie," their dad said. "You

did all the work by writing the poem and entering the contest all on your own. Now you're a finalist."

"But I'll have to read my poem out loud in front of a lot of strangers," Lily said.

"We'll be there to cheer you on," said Daisy. "We may be strange, but we're not strangers."

Lily tried to smile, but it didn't work. "You know what happens when I get nervous."

Violet nodded. "You get the . . ."

"Hic, hic, hiccups," said Lily, covering her mouth.

"Well, it may not happen then," said Daisy.

"You can do it," said their dad. "And we'll all be there to root for you. Right, Trouble, old boy?"

"*Arf, arf.*"

"Hic, hic."

The Divines gave Lily her space. They didn't talk about the contest, and Lily practiced reading her poem in private. Daisy and Violet snuck upstairs and listened outside their bedroom door. Lily sounded great. So far, so good.

Somehow, when Saturday morning rolled around, Lily didn't feel nervous at all. She wore her favorite pink top and denim skirt.

Helen Divine tied a bright-red neckerchief on Trouble.

Violet brushed his gold-and-white coat until it shone.

Daisy had even brushed Trouble's teeth.

Everyone piled into the car. They listened to relaxing music throughout the ride.

"We're almost there," Herb Divine said, making a final turn.

"I told Grandma Rose we'll save some seats," Helen Divine said. "She's picking up Grandpa Dash."

"But it's not a date," their father added.

Violet and Daisy laughed. They looked at Lily, who sat silently in the middle.

Suddenly Lily yelled, "Stop the car!"

"What?" their parents said.

"Lily has to vomit," Violet said, edging away from her.

Daisy leaned back in the other direction.

Lily shook her head. "It's worse than that," she said.

"Worse than vomiting?" said Daisy.

"I left the poem at home," Lily wailed. "It's on my bed."

"Oh, dear," their mother said as their father pulled up to the Dandy Dog Training School. "I should have made sure you had it with you."

"I can't go on," Lily moaned.

"Yes, you can," said Daisy. "I heard you saying the poem in your sleep. You were so loud, you almost drowned out Violet's snoring. Trust me, you know all the words by heart."

"No, I don't," said Lily, crossing her arms.

"Yes, you do," said Violet, tugging on her elbow. "And I don't snore."

"Arf, arf."

"Do it for Trouble," Daisy said.

Lily reached behind her, and Trouble licked her hand. She swallowed and nodded.

"Arf, arf!"

There were two other finalists besides Lily. One of them was the tallest man she had ever seen. He even towered over his enormous black-and-white Great Dane. At first Lily thought it was a horse walking past her. While the man read his poem, his dog, Tiny, sat like a quiet, gentle giant. The other finalist was a woman with a pink-and-purple polka-dot bow placed on top of her curly white hair. Her fluffy white poodle wore a bow to match. When the woman took her turn, her little dog, Spike, yipped and yapped the entire time. Lily thought both dogs looked a bit like their owners.

She didn't think she looked like Trouble, except for their blue eyes.

Lily sat frozen in the front row the entire time. Trouble was with her family. She didn't dare turn around and look at them. When her name was called, she stood up slowly and walked to the microphone on trembling legs. She stood stiffly with her hands behind her back, clasping her sweaty palms.

She opened her mouth to speak, but no words came out, just a little hiccup. Lily clamped her mouth shut. She looked into the audience and saw her family. Grandma Rose waved.

Lily opened her mouth to try again. "Hic, hic, our dog is, hic, hic." Her voice shook. She would never get through the poem. Lily wished she could sink into the ground and disappear completely. Then she heard footsteps. It was Violet leading Trouble down the aisle. Lily kept her eyes trained on Trouble's friendly, furry face as he bounded toward her.

"Stay," Violet said to Trouble. "That goes for you, too," she whispered to Lily.

Lily looked down at Trouble, and he looked up at her. She cleared her throat and began reciting the poem. Lily didn't have a clue what she said, but somehow she got through it, hiccups and all.

When she finished, everyone applauded. Lily bent down to Trouble and told him to take a bow. And he did.

The Divine family rushed up and gathered around Lily and Trouble.

"Way to go Lily," her sisters said.

"We're so proud of you," said her parents.

"As your grandpa Dash would say, you were simply splendid," said Grandma Rose.

"And as for Trouble," said Grandpa Dash, "I'd call that a Divine bow-wow!"

Before Lily could catch her breath, it was announced that all three finalists were winners.

The tall man won a gigantic case of dog food for his Great Dane. The woman with the polka-dot bow won a day of grooming at the pet spa for her poodle. And Lily's prize was the five free training lessons for Trouble.

The training coupons were in the shape of big dog biscuits. Lily leaned forward and showed them to Trouble. "These are all yours," she said.

The Divines burst out laughing as Trouble sniffed the biscuit-shaped coupons and began chewing away.